FIFTEEN AND CHANGE

MAX HOWARD

An imprint of Enslow Publishing

WEST **44** BOOKS™

Please visit our website, www.west44books.com.
For a free color catalog of all our high-quality books,
call toll free 1-800-542-2595 or fax 1-877-542-2596.

Cataloging-in-Publication Data

Names: Howard, Max.
Title: Fifteen and change / Max Howard.
Description: New York : West 44, 2019. | Series: West 44
YA verse Identifiers: ISBN 9781538382592 (pbk.) | ISBN
9781538382608 (library bound) | ISBN 9781538383308
(ebook) Subjects: LCSH: Children's poetry, American. |
Children's poetry, English. | English poetry. Classification:
LCC PS586.3 F548 2019 | DDC 811'.60809282--dc23

First Edition

Published in 2019 by
Enslow Publishing LLC
101 West 23rd Street, Suite #240
New York, NY 10011

Copyright © 2019 Enslow Publishing LLC

Editor: Caitie McAneney
Designer: Seth Hughes

Printed in the United States of America

CPSIA compliance information: Batch #CS18W44: For further information contact
Enslow Publishing LLC, New York, New York at 1-800-542-2595.

To hope and all things with feathers

Focus.
Remember what it felt like to be
invisible.

Teacher looks around the room.
He's going to call on somebody.

I've done it before.
Think.
Focus.

Turning Invisible

All during math class
I try to be invisible.

Focus.
Remember
what works.
Remember hunting deer
with Dad in the tree stand.
Quiet. Still.

The teacher's eyes flick over me
like he doesn't see me,
like I'm invisible.

Teacher calls on some girl:
Sarah, what do you think?

Every Girl at This New School

is named Sarah.

At my old school
back in Blue Way, Wisconsin,
all the girls were Maddie.
All the boys were Jake.

All the boys here are Jake, too.
People think my name is Jake.
It's not.
It's Zeke.
Sometimes Zekers.

Mom's New Boyfriend

I wish Paul
would just
swear.

But he's
Christian
so he won't.

Instead
he calls my mom a
BRITCH.

He says
it's a joke.
Her name is Britney.
Brit.
Britch.
Get it?

My mom laughs.
Paul says,
Shut up,
you dumb britch.

Close the door to your room.
Lie down.
Keep the light off.
Pretend you're not there.

Pretend you don't hear Paul's
video game sounds.
Shooting.
Explosions.
He's playing *CS:Go* on Steam.

Paul gets mad.
Yells at the computer,

Oh, you little britch.
Britch, I'm gonna kill you.

How to Disappear on a Boat

One night Dad and I took the canoe out.
The air was cold.
The water was warm.
Fog rolled off the lake.
It hung so thick between us
I couldn't see my dad.
He couldn't see me.

I sometimes forget what he looks like now.
I have to go on Facebook to find his picture.
He lives back in Wisconsin.
He posts a lot of selfies,
sometimes with a fish.

My Profile Pic

is someone else.

Godzilla
from the 70s.

I delete all my selfies.
I don't mind being red haired,
skinny,
freckled,
fourteen and a half.

I mind having my picture taken.
I mind being seen.

I'd never ridden a city bus.
Cars, yes.
School bus, yes.
Trucks, yes.
Tractors, yes.
Snowmobiles.
Four-wheelers.

I'd never been inside an apartment.
Houses, yes.
Trailers, yes.
Boats, yes.
Campers, RVs.
Tents, barns, pole sheds.
Ice shanties.
Never an apartment.

If all apartments are like Paul's apartment,
then apartments
smell like hot dog water.

Silverfish squirm
in the bathtub.

The sink burps.
The couch farts.

Or else it's Paul
sitting there
eating string cheese.

Like Butterflies

The vacuum broke at the motel.
My mom didn't want to tell her boss.
He might make her pay for it.
So she picked up
lint
hair
Cheetos
with her fingers.

But she got to watch
Say Yes to the Dress
while cleaning the rooms.

She says, *Some of these brides are so
beautiful—*
like butterflies.

*I wanted to feel
like a butterfly.*

Or

My teeth hurt.

Or

Paul loves me.

Or

He doesn't.

Payday Lending

When Mom can't pay the loan,
they'll take the car.

Then how are we supposed to get home?
I mean *home,*
to Blue Way, Wisconsin.
To the lake, the woods?

But rent, Zekers, she says.

Rent.

My Mom Is Beautiful But

her breath stinks.

Her cheek is red, hot, and puffy.
I bring ice.

She drinks rum. Says,
My tooth hurts.

No money to go to the dentist.

Not my problem, says Paul.

Losing the Car Is One Thing

Losing a tooth is another.
Mom went to the dentist instead.
Didn't pay on her loan.

She lost a car to lose a tooth.
Now she hides her smile.
Covers her mouth with her hand.

We're watching
Say Yes to the Dress.
Some of those brides are so beautiful,
like butterflies.

Mom's voice is muffled.
She talks behind her
hand, takes the bus to work.

Money Honey

I bring Mom tissues,
ice, rum.

You're so helpful,
Mom says. She
wipes her eyes,
smiles behind her hand.

Now.
Say it
now:
Mom, why don't we just move back to Wisconsin?

She says,
It's the money, honey.

HELP WANTED

My heart pounds
like I've spotted a deer.

Breathe in,
smell pizza.
Breathe out,
phones are ringing.
Will that be for pickup or delivery?

Breathe in,
What would you like on that?
Breathe out,
try not to be
invisible.

Say:

Hey, I saw your sign outside.
You guys hiring?

The Manager's Office

is not fancy.
Ripped up old chairs,
papers everywhere,
pizza sauce fingerprints
all over the light switch.

The manager's mouth
hides behind his beard.
He pinches a banana pepper
between his fingers.
Shoves it into all that beard.
Crunches.
Wipes his hand on his pants.

Hi, I'm Scott.

Job Interview

My mouth
is moving.
I'm saying
something.

But I can't hear it.

My voice is soft.
My stomach is growling.
(I'm always starving after school.)

Today
my hunger is louder
than my voice.

First Day at Work

Hi, I'm Olivia. I'll give you the tour.
She spreads her arms wide,
spins around.
Her red hair is like flames around her face.

I pretend to understand what she's saying.

Dry storage.

Dumpster.

Prep area.

We stand in the walk-in freezer.
I can see my breath,
but I could never be cold around Olivia.

Fire Girl

Olivia
sticks a long hook into the ovens,
pops the bubbles
rising
in the pizza crusts.

Wild red hair
like a prairie fire.
But a mouth
like a rosebud
that blooms
when she smiles.

She says,
Zeke, huh?
You look more like a Zekers.

My heart melts
like cheese on a pizza.

She called me Zekers.

Heat broke.

Landlord
isn't answering his phone.
Plus, the power
got cut off.

Britch, you were supposed to pay the bill.

They're fighting,
wearing hats and coats,
using phone flashlights
like candles.
The light makes their faces
look blue.

is what I want to say.

But Paul's got his hands
in Mom's coat pockets
looking for change.

Mom squirms,
tries out a normal voice.
Zeke, you're home late today.
Everything OK?

I lie:
Sorry.
Got detention.

I'm Going to Get Paid

And I'm not going to let Paul
take my money.
I'm going to hide it.

I stand on my bed,
reach up and
slide apart
the ceiling tiles.

I'll cash my checks and
hide the bills up here.

Then one day
I'll open the ceiling.
It'll rain money on Mom and me.

We Need a Car

if we're going to move back
to Blue Way.

A car to get there.
A car to get around in.
There are no buses out there.

In study hall I look online
for something cheap but reliable.

About $3,000 will do it.

Also we need first month's rent.
Security deposit.

Say, $2,000.

We Need $5,000

I will make $7.25 an hour
and work 18 hours a week.

In 38.31 weeks
I will have $5,000.

Math is easy
when you want
something.

First Day at Casa de Pizza

They'll take the cost of my
green uniform
out of my first check.

So now I'll have to work even longer.
Just to get to $5,000.

I think about what a year
looks like while
folding pizza boxes.

Christmas lights.
Easter eggs.
Fireworks.
Jack-o'-lanterns.
Thanksgiving turkeys.

Did you know
you can get paper cuts
from cardboard?

Check the Schedule

Dylan trains me.

Double-bag the trash
so it doesn't leak.
Drop a germ-killing
tablet in the sink.

Dylan is a senior at my school.
He has a tiny beard.
He shows me how to check the work schedule.

I won't work with Olivia again for a week.

Scott Is on a Diet

He used to eat pizza,
Dylan says.
Now he eats banana peppers.

Two yellow peppers
go in a corner
of each box.
I check to make sure
before each pizza goes out.

You know Scott's
standing behind you
watching you
because you hear him crunching.

CRUNCH CRUNCH CRUNCH

What, kid, did you get your period?

Scott is crunching and laughing.
He points at the floor.

The trash bag has burst and
I'm dragging a red line
of tomato sauce
all across the floor.

Olivia, look. Kid got his first period.

I turn as red as the sauce.

First Paycheck

It's less than I thought.
Taxes. Social security.
Plus the check-cashing place
takes a cut.

I slide five twenties
into an old envelope.
Slip it into my hiding spot
in the ceiling.

That's when I hear the

SLAP.

It Doesn't Leave a Mark

My mom's face looks fine.
But the sound of the slap,
my mom's gasp.
Those sounds
left a mark in my mind.

It's OK.
I'll get us home.
I just need to make money faster.

on a day she's
supposed to work.

That's how I learn
she's in college.

She's arguing with Scott.

I asked off, she says.

Crunch. Crunch.
Not my problem, he says.

Does she know I'm still in high school?
Yesterday she threw an olive and
I caught it in my mouth.

She said,
Zekers for the win!

Pizza Prep

Dylan showed me
how to refill plastic
Cambro containers
with chopped
mushrooms and
peppers.

But now Mary
who isn't even a manager—
just THINKS she is—
told me I was cutting the
peppers
mushrooms
onions
wrong.

When she ducked out to smoke,
I thought about locking the door.

This School Has Open Campus Lunch

We have 50 minutes.
We can go anywhere we want.
It's amazing.

Most kids
go across the street
to Taco Bell
or KFC.

I go to the park,
vanish
into the trees.

I climb
to the top
of a tall
pine and
eat.

Everything is green,
fresh, and crisp.
Except my Cheetos,
which are orange.

Bud, the Pizza Delivery Driver

looks like a sea captain
with a long
white beard.

Probably about 100 years old,
he smokes a pipe
in his old Honda
when he's not
out on delivery runs.

Olivia says Bud looks like Santa.
But Dylan says
Bud used to be a doctor.
Until he got fired
for keeping
dead bodies
in his freezer
at home.

with her ponytail.

Her long brown hair
goes all the way to her butt.

When we get slammed
with lots of pizza orders
she whips around fast,
her ponytail smacking into people.

She hollers,
LET'S SHOW SOME HUSTLE, PEOPLE.

Bud won't hustle.
When Mary yells,
he says,
Bud don't budge, baby.

whenever we get slammed.

Dylan complains about it.

Mary says, *I'm going to tell Scott you said that.*

When she leaves, Dylan says,
Mary's a thirty-five-year-old tattletale.

Olivia says,
Be kind—
she has a hard life.

Dylan says,
Easy for you to say, Olivia.

Olivia gasps
like he's slapped her.

I Like Working with Timothy

He's older than Mary
and he's black.
There aren't many black people
back in Blue Way,
so at first I was nervous:
What if I said
the wrong thing?

But right away
we get in a rhythm.
Me sprinkling cheese.
Him doing toppings.
It's nice, quiet.

I wonder if he knows
what Dylan said and why
it hurt Olivia's feelings.

Yesterday Dylan High-Fived Me

in the hall at school.
His beard
is thin and his teeth are big
and when he smiles,
everyone looks.
It's like a light
just came on.

Now
guys I don't even know
nod at me
in the hall.

I worry
I'll nod
wrong, somehow.

So I walk looking up,
counting
the ceiling tiles.

because I get to eat them.

Whenever I get hungry,
I wait for someone to order
a plain cheese pizza.
Then I put pepperoni and olives on it
as if by mistake.

I hide behind the folded pizza boxes
stacked to the ceiling.

It's like I'm invisible.

No one notices me eating
slice after slice.

because she has a second
job now.
She's a waitress
at an old folks' home.

She's too tired
to ask questions
about Nature Club,
which is good
because Nature Club
doesn't exist.
It's where I tell her I go
instead of work.

She doesn't ask me any questions at all.

She's busy
using a fine-tooth comb
to scratch gunk
off Paul's scalp
while he makes
monkey noises.

You've Got to Work on Your Cheese Lock, Mister

Mary tells me.

She shows me how
to build a dam
out of shredded cheese
to keep pizza sauce
from leaking
during delivery.

Her fingers
are red.
(Her other job is a
motel maid.
It's hard on the hands.)

But I can tell sprinkling white cheese
makes her happy.
It's like a snow globe, she says.

I Splurge

Spend a little money from my second
Casa de Pizza paycheck
on udder balm.

Dairy farmers use it.
It's good for chapped hands.

I leave it in Mom's purse.
Her hands are red and cracked, too.

She thinks it's a present from Paul.

I don't say anything.
I have $290 in the ceiling.

Closing

Olivia shows me
how to take down the cold bar.

I wash the prep tubs.
She does the books.

When she locks up,
the keys jingle.

I ask,
How much did we take in tonight, anyway?

Five thousand,
she says.
Flips off the lights.

Five thousand
in
one
night!

I stand there in the dark
doing the math in my head.

Venison

Timothy brought me a pound of
venison. A plastic bag
full of fresh deer meat.

We roasted it in the oven,
made a venison pizza.

It tasted like Wisconsin.

Fair to the Deer

Timothy hunts in the
state forest.
Drives two hours
in his old Toyota truck.

He hunts
with a bow and arrow.
Says it's more
fair
to the deer
than a gun.

I picture him in the woods.
Gray dreadlocks blending into
a misty morning.

He holds his breath.
His arrow flies
through the silver woods.

Surprise

One night when I get home from work
stuffed with pepperoni and olive
mistakes, I find Mom dancing around.

I got a big tip today,
she says.
So I ordered you a pizza!

I pretend to be excited.

Hide behind the couch
in case Bud's
the delivery driver.

Olivia's Brand-New Tattoo

She pulls her shirt
off her shoulder and
shows me.

A red rose
in a loop
of black letters.

I lean close.
Olivia smells like
cinnamon. And the rose
is as red as Olivia's
hair. The letters are
cursive.

*I can't read
cursive*, I tell her.

Bread and roses,
she says.
It's a song.

Illegal

I'm hiding behind a tower
of pizza boxes,
eating.

Scott and Dylan don't know I'm there.

Have her call me if she wants a job,
says Scott. *What's her name?*

Hannah, says Dylan.
Hannah Torres Bravo.
She's my cousin.

Hannah. Huh,
Scott says.
That sounds like an American name.
I thought she was an illegal?

CRUNCH CRUNCH CRUNCH

Whatever.
Not my problem.

Hey kid.

CRUNCH CRUNCH CRUNCH

Go train Hannah on trash duty,
says Scott.

Make sure to show her to double-bag,
says Mary.

Hannah doesn't say anything.
She is so small and so quiet,
I forget she's there.

I let a door close in her face
on the way to the alley.

Does Your Cousin Speak English?

Olivia asks.

Hannah? Of course, says Dylan.

I've just never heard her speak.
Olivia runs a pizza cutter
through a large pie.
Closes the box lid.

She's quiet, Dylan says.
He points at me.
Like him.

I jump.

I didn't realize
he noticed me
mopping quietly
behind the ovens.

The Mouse

Mary has it by the tail.
Swings it around.
Scott! Look what I found!
And someone's been feeding him!

The mouse squirms.
Mary's ponytail shakes.

Someone made a little nest for him
in dry storage,
kept him as a pet.

She whips toward me,
ponytail flying.
Mouse flying.

Was it you?

The Nest

is a mouse heaven.

A little house
made of a pizza box
tucked on a warm, dry shelf.

Napkin bed.
Soda bottle lid
for a water dish.
Even a tiny pizza,
special baked.

Crust the size of a
quarter.

Dot of sauce.

Extra cheese.

CRUNCH CRUNCH CRUNCH

You'll get us shut down
by the health department,
Scott yells.

Still chewing,
he knocks the mouse house
off the shelf.
Stomps it.

Yeah, who did this?
Mary echoes,
shakes the mouse.

Stop, you'll break its spine!
Olivia cries.
Put it in a to-go cup.
I'll release it into the wild.

on a fresh round of dough
and wonder who made the mouse house.
Who kept a pet at work?

Timothy loves nature,
is a careful worker.
He could make a perfect tiny pizza.

Or Dylan.
His thin beard
looks like a mouse's
whiskers.

Olivia cried.

Hannah is so quiet.
Who knows what
she could do?

Snap!

In the middle of the night,
I hear a
SNAP!

It wakes me up.

Then it's quiet,
just normal sounds.

The heater,
Paul's snore,
chunky as cottage cheese.

I go back to sleep.

Breakfast

Paul tricks Mom.
Finds a dead mouse
in one of the traps.
That explains the snap.
Drops it in her coffee.

She takes a sip and
her lips touch fur.

Dead fur.
A cold tail.

She screams.
Paul laughs.

I have $500 in the ceiling.

The Snow Looks Like Shooting Stars

Olivia says.
The outside world is white and wild.
But inside
the pizza ovens are so hot.

Olivia wears a tank top.
Shows off her rose tattoo.

I slide breadsticks out of the oven.
Say, *Hey, Olivia.*
Breadsticks and roses?

She laughs.

It feels like shooting stars.

I'm Frozen Up to the Eyeballs

Waiting alone
for the bus.

Suddenly a black BMW SUV
pulls over.

The tinted window slides down.

It's Olivia at the wheel.
Get in, Zekers.
I'm giving you a ride home.

I Don't Feel Invisible

in the BMW.
I feel bulletproof.

Like a powerful beast.

Leather seats.
Purring engine.

Sleek and fast,
we pass
McDonald's,
Payday Loans,
the motel
where Mom works.

Sleek and fast,
it's like we own the world.
We killed it.
We crushed it.
It's ours.

Don't Tell Anyone About This, OK?

I don't want Dylan or Scott
to know
this car is mine,
says Olivia.

That's why I always park it
down the block.

My parents bought it.

They have money.

It's awkward.

If it were up to me,
I'd drive a Prius.

Cold Picnic, Hot Chocolate

At lunch
I pull the earflaps
down on my cap,
go to the park,
climb to the top
of my tree.

It's freezing cold and
I only have a banana.

But when I climb down,
someone's left me a
hot chocolate.

Who?

The cocoa's so warm,
the cup melted a circle
in the snow.

Christmas Then, Christmas Now

In Blue Way,
we used to drive
out to a Christmas tree farm
on the lake.
Blasts of wind blew snow
across the ice.
It was always snowing
in the Christmas woods.

Now Mom and I walk
to the Rite Aid parking lot.
I feel bad for the cut pine trees.
Leaning up against a camper.
Breathing in car fumes.
Plastic bags and old candy wrappers
dancing at their feet.

Christmas at Work

Scott wears a red Santa hat.
Says, *Yeah right!*
when Dylan asks about a
Christmas bonus.

Then the hat goes missing.
Scott searches the girls' purses.
But he doesn't notice
when Bud walks in
from a delivery
wearing it.

With his long white beard,
Bud just naturally
looks like Santa.

sends me
a $50
bill.

Just that.

No card.

Just *Merry Christmas,* Z
in blue ink
on the cash.

Not Zekers.
Not even Zeke.
Just Z.

I want to tear
the money into
tiny pieces.

Throw them
in the snow.

Instead I put the $50
in the ceiling.

She has flour on her shirt.
A dab of red sauce
on her forehead.
Red lipstick.

Was it your mouse?

She laughs.

*I was going to
ask you the same thing, Zekers.*

Mary Has a Bad Cough

It sounds like she swallowed a goose.

Honk honk honk

But who can afford
a sick day?

She has three kids
so she always has a cold.

When she makes pizza
her cough blows the cheese shreds
everywhere.
Like a broken snow globe.

Hannah's Superpower

She's small and quiet,
but she can turn a hunk of dough
into a perfect pizza round
in less than 30 seconds.

That's faster than me.
Faster than Timothy.
Faster than Dylan.
Faster than Mary.

Even Scott tried to beat her.
When he lost,
he gave her a coupon
for free breadsticks.

The Best Thing About Winter

is riding shotgun
in Olivia's black
BMW.

It rides so smooth
it seems to float
over the snowy streets,
over the potholes,
home to Paul's apartment.

When I get home,
I take off my shoes.
Tiptoe
so Mom doesn't notice
I'm home late.

Would you rather
eat skinny snake poop
or make out with your math teacher
in front of everyone?

Which do you like best:
sweet or salty?
oceans or mountains?

What is best to have:
power or love?

Love.

Hannah Goes Wild

She's so quiet.
Dark hair falling over her eyes.
No one notices her take
a bottle of Sprite
from the cooler and
shake it up.

Dylan walks in.

Hannah unscrews the cap,
blasts him with fizz, saying,
Congratulations!!!

He got his first college acceptance.
We all clap.

Until Mary says,
This is time theft, guys.
Get back to work.

Mom Finally Opened My Report Card

after letting it sit
and sit
under the bills
and get
syrup on it.

So now she cares.
Now she
wants to know
why I'm always gone.
Where I go.
What I do.
If I'm on drugs.

Paul pins me up against
the fridge,
squishes me
with his belly.

Listen, you little son of a britch.
Don't. You. Upset. Her.

Smiling Pizza

On Fridays
Timothy makes a pepperoni
smiley face pizza
because on weekends
he sees his daughter.

She's eight.

Once Hannah carved a green pepper
nose,
stuck it in the middle of the pie.

It made the pizza look almost
human.

When I Get Home

Paul and Mom
have their paws
in my dresser drawer.

We wouldn't have to snoop,
Mom says,
if you would just
tell me
where you go.
Who drives you
in that fancy car?

I Want to Tell Mom I Have a Job

She'd be proud.
But I don't want Paul
to get my money.

Zekers, I'm asking you a question!
Mom yells.

Shut up, britch,
I snap.

The worst part is:
Mom shuts up.

In werewolf movies
it hurts
when the beast
breaks through the man's
human skin.

But turning into Paul
doesn't feel
like anything at all.

I feel like
Paul and it's
like
nothing.

On Monday

Timothy says
his daughter didn't want to eat
that pizza
with the green pepper
nose.

She wanted to sleep with it
in her bed.

Hannah smiles.
Bounces on her tiptoes,
happy.

I wish I could turn up
the volume
on their happiness.

It's like music
my werewolf heart
can barely hear.

Olivia's Secret

The BMW
purrs.

Bun warmer?
says Olivia,
pressing a button
for seat heat.

I wonder
for the millionth time:
If Olivia
is so rich,
why does she work at Casa de Pizza?

It's like she can read minds.

Zekers,
do you want to know a secret?
I'm salting in.

Salting In

is when
someone gets a job
at a place
just to
stir things up.

Help people.
Organize.
Fight for:

better wages,
sick days,
health insurance.

It's like being a spy.
A secret agent,
except without
cool gadgets
and with
trash duty.

Work Party at Olivia's House

The house used to be fancy
100 years ago.
Now it's a wreck, a
filthy nest
for 12 college kids.

They're all
salting in
at fast food places.

The furniture's all
been stolen
from lawns and dumpsters.

Olivia hops up
on a stained couch,
yells,
Welcome!
I invited you here tonight
because what's happening at Casa de Pizza
ain't right!

Low pay.

No sick days.

No health insurance.

Scott will cut your hours
if you call in sick
or bug him.

Plus he drops mushrooms
down the girls'
shirts.

Says, *Why don't you like me?*
I'm a fungi!
Get it?
he says.

Fun guy?

Olivia the Firefly

Olivia glows
floats
sings.

We make the pizza.
We turn flour and tomatoes
into money.

We have the power.

Without us,
there's no pizza.
If we stick together,
we can do anything.
We can win.

They're paying $15
an hour now in
Seattle.
Why not
here?

this whole time,
I'd already be home
in Blue Way.

Driving my car across
the center of the lake
where it's frozen thick.

I'd pull up next
to my dad's
ice shanty.

We'd sit inside,
fish
through a hole
in the ice.

Fried panfish
is better
than pizza.

cleaning,
maybe she would never
have felt stuck
with Paul in the first place.

Never would say,
But Zekers,
where else we gonna go?

Zekers, You In?

Olivia asks.

Fifteen dollars an hour?
HELL YES!
I say.

My voice is so loud
I almost jump.

I catch sight of myself
in the dirty glass
above the fireplace.

Have I gotten taller?

You Don't Know What You're Asking

Dylan stands up,
kicks the
rug with the toe
of his boot.

If Scott finds out
we're asking for more money,
he'll fire us.

Unlike you, Olivia,
I need this job
if I'm gonna pay for school.

It's Illegal

to fire you for joining a union,
Olivia says.
That doesn't mean
Scott won't try.
It just means he
won't win.

Win?
says Timothy.
I don't want to win.
I want to feed my kid.

My heart is pounding
so loud
I can barely hear him.

I want to win.
For once.
So bad.

Wild Creature

I leave Olivia's party
feeling like a vampire
in a movie.
Strong.
Changed.

The world
outside
sparkles.

Every branch
on every tree
looks sharp.

The snowflakes
fall, wet and fat.
I can see the tiny
crystal shapes.

I'm in the city
but I feel like a
wild creature
prowling the woods.

everything is blurry:

Mom's eye makeup.
(She's crying.)

The kitchen table.
(There's milk
spilled
      all over it.)

Mom's arms.
(A purple blur
of finger marks
where Paul
shook her.)

Even I
feel blurry.

My spine
feels melty.
My legs, too.
I have to sit down.

There's milk
on the chair.

Wet Pants

It's not how I want to see
Paul.
With a stain
like I peed myself
on my pants.

He's whistling.
Grabbing a pudding cup
from the fridge
while the milk drips
off the table.

He acts like
he doesn't see me.

I say.
She hides behind
a tissue,
acts like
she doesn't hear me.

I go to my room,
check the ceiling.
I have $1,290.

It's not enough.

I need more
NOW.

No time to fight
for better pay someday.

No time to win one
just to win one.

I need money now.

Olivia Smiles at Me

but I ignore her.
Walk right past the
prep area
past the ovens
back to Scott's office.

Olivia is so surprised
she drips
pizza sauce
on the counter.

Scott, I say.
I need more hours.
I need more money.

CRUNCH CRUNCH CRUNCH

OK,
says Scott.
It'll have to be
under the table
though, because
you're not eighteen.

Mary coughs.
Blood flies out,
makes a red splat
on the white counter.

Scott stands there,
crunching.

Says,
Yuck, throat pizza!
Clean it up.
Get a bleach rag.

Mary's face
looks like
a bleach rag.
Damp and gray.

Bud comes in,
takes five pizzas
out for delivery.

Bread and Roses

I spent $15.

Three red roses.
One white loaf
of Wonderbread.

I hide them
in my backpack.
Stick my backpack
in the walk-in cooler
while I work
to keep the roses fresh.

My backpack's
full of bread and roses.
I play with the zipper
while Olivia drives me home.
She pulls over
near Paul's apartment,
puts the BMW in park.
(She never does that.)
Turns off the engine.
Unbuckles her seatbelt.
Looks at me.

I can feel my heart
in my whole body.

I'm Just Worried About You, Zekers

Olivia says.

Is everything OK?
Why haven't you been coming
to the fifteen-dollar-an-hour
organizing meetings?

She sounds like Mom.
Questions, questions.

I squeeze my backpack
so hard
a thorn
from a rose inside
pricks me.

I just changed my mind,
I say.

I leave
without
giving Olivia
anything.

At First I Think the House Is on Fire

Then I see
it's just candles.
Led Zeppelin and
candles.
They're crowded on the
coffee table,
lined up
along the back
of the couch.

The smoke alarm's
screaming.
I smell frozen pizza
burning.

Mom's laughing.

Paul's swinging her
around.

Her feet fly out,
knock a candle
onto a red pillow.

Valentine's Day, Part Three

Paul sings about
stairways and heaven,
spinning Mom
around the room.

I stamp the fire out
of the pillow.

Zekers! Mom screams.
We're getting married!
Paul proposed.

They whirl.
Dangerous,
candlelit.

I take the pizza out.
It's burned black.
I open the window,
fan the smoke.

The flowers wilt
in my backpack.
Mom's rock
scratches my nose
when she shoves
her ring
in my face.

Isn't it beautiful?
I feel
like a princess.
See? It's
princess cut.
My favorite!

I don't know much
about diamonds.
But I know
this wedding
is a bad idea.

so I can use the office phone
to call Dad.
It's a long shot,
but maybe
he can stop this wedding
or ask me
to live with him.

A woman answers, says,
I just got this number.
I don't know your dad.
Sorry.

When I hang up,
the secretary says,
Honey, you look green,
and sends me to the nurse.

was so spiky
it poked a hole
in her glove
at work.

All the other motel maids
saw the
sparkle.

They stole
wine and chocolates
from the Honeymoon Suite
cupboard.
Sang, *Here comes the bride.*

I felt so
beautiful,
Mom says.

Olivia Makes a New Friend

When Hannah
draws something
on the inside
of a pizza box,
Olivia says,
Oh my god,
Hannah,
you're the best.

They both go quiet
when Bud
comes in.
He scoops up some pizzas
to deliver.

His white beard is stained
yellow from his pipe.
His freezer is maybe full
of dead bodies.

You Want to Make Some Money

Don't you, kid?
Scott says, crunching.

Take all
Mary's hours.
You'll work cash
under the table
to get around
the kiddie labor laws.

I think about Mary's
whipping ponytail and
red coughs.
What about Mary?
I ask.

Scott shrugs.
Mary missed a shift.
So I'm cutting all her
hours this week.

I Am Spinning Dough into a Crust

when Mary shows up
in her uniform
ready to work.
Tossing her ponytail.
Yelling:
Dylan! Get a broom!

Scott snaps his fingers,
yells
with his mouth full:

*Mary! I told you
you're 86'd.
This is the kid's shift now.
He's working for you
all this week.
Kid, show Mary the door.*

Throwing Mary Out

I wipe my flour hands
on my apron.
Watch my shoes
walking behind Mary's shoes
out the front door.

She lights a smoke.
Her hands shake.
Even her ponytail shakes.

I just stand there
shivering.
Wanting
to say
I'm sorry.
But before I can,
she says,

It's not your problem.

My Problem

is Olivia's silence
when she drives me home.

My problem

is Mom
wiggling her fingers
like butterfly wings,
showing off her ring.

My problem

is Paul
being Paul.

My problem

is Dad
being totally AWOL.
Completely disappearing,
maybe forever.

My problem
is money.
A mom who doesn't want
to go back to Blue Way.

My Birthday

Mom writes
15 in grape jelly
on my toast.
Promises to cook me
a special supper.

I already have plans,
I tell her.
Even though
my plans are just
to throw some dough
with Olivia
at Casa.

Mom wiggles
her eyebrows:
Zekers, are you meeting a girl?

Yes,
I say.

Not exactly lying.

of King Meat pizzas.

Olivia counts out
his change:
*That's thirteen, fourteen,
fifteen aaaaand
change.*

The man
traps her hands
with his.

Pulls her halfway
across the counter.
Kisses her neck
like an old
octopus.

Scott just stands there
crunching.
I just stand there
letting the mop drip.

Payday

is huge.
I made $210.75 in cash
because I took
Mary's shifts.

I stand on
tiptoes
on my bed.

Tilt the ceiling tiles.
Reach inside to
add to my stash
of cash.

But my hands
touch empty air.
I feel around
in the tall
darkness.

But it's gone.
My money is gone.

Mom's Diamond Winks

in a pool of soap suds
next to the sink.
Mom, I say.
Did you or Paul
take my money?

She says,
Why would you say a thing like that?

But she hides
the ring
with the sponge.
She won't look
at me.
So I know.

They did it.
Took my money.
Bought a ring.

Just peels
thin strips
of string
cheese, drips
them into his
mouth.

Way I see it,
he says.
It's my house.
So everything in it
belongs to me.

He unpeels
another white
cheese stick. Says,

It's impossible
for me to steal
anything from anyone
who lives here.

Mom's Speech

You're gone
all the time.
Who knows where.
A fancy car
drops you off.
You hide
thousands of dollars
in your room.
Plus two Ds
on your report card.

Drugs are a big NO, mister.
I love you.
This is tough
love,
honey.

She slides her soapy ring
back on her finger.

Olivia's housemate says.
He has a long
black beard.
Olivia, what if his mom calls the cops?
You have to think about
the movement.
He crosses
his arms over his
chest so his
muscles look bigger.

Just for tonight,
Olivia says.
She unrolls a sleeping bag
on the dining room floor.

Beard guy stomps off.

Olivia and I Are Alone

in the empty
dining room.
She's in her PJs
and I'm in a blue bag.

What? she asks.
I swallow.
The heater
clangs.

I want to say one thing.
But I say something else:
What does bread and roses mean?

It's from a song that changed the world,
Olivia says.

A hundred years ago
the bosses locked the workers
inside the factory
to control them.

Then the factory caught fire.
The workers burned.

A woman named Rose
got all the workers together.
They went on strike.
Asked for better pay.

And not just better pay.
For safety.
Respect.
Dignity.

They wanted bread and also roses.

Olivia Takes My Hand

She brings it to the rose tattoo
on her arm.
Her skin is warm.

She says,

The striking
workers
carried signs saying,

The worker must have bread,
but she must have roses, too.

We have a right
to good wages and respect.

Today
we fight with them.
With those workers
who fought for us.

the heater roars.
My blood, too.
I'm touching her tattoo
with my fingertips
in the dark.

Then suddenly she's zipping
up her sweatshirt.
Pushing me away, saying,
Good night, Zekers.
Sorry to get so intense.
I'm just a history nerd.

She's gone.
My heart bangs
louder
than the heater.

I Don't Sleep and I Can't Calm Down

Not until biology class.
I like bio.
Mr. Leo never calls on random kids
and I know a lot about plants and animals.

Plus today it's just coloring
a flower diagram. As I turn
plant parts pink,
my heart slows down.

I don't want to go home.
But sleeping at Olivia's—
it's like slamming Red Bulls
and pixie sticks.
It's too much.

Most Improved

Things will get better,
Mom promises
when I come home.

Once
in Blue Way
teachers voted me
Most Improved Student.

It didn't feel
like a compliment.

But Paul is now
Most Improved Paul.

He's working
night security
at a hospital.
He's always gone
or sleeping.

Beach Day

It's five below
so Mom
blasts the Beach Boys and
bakes a Jiffy cake.

While it cools
on the counter
she opens the oven door
so the heat flows out,
rolls over us.

We take off our shoes and
go barefoot
while she cranks open
a can of pineapple,
saying,
Aloha. Welcome to Hawaii.

Just Because

Mom and Paul
are engaged
doesn't mean
it's going to
work out.

Mom and Dad
WERE MARRIED.
Now Dad is gone.

Maybe Paul will go, too.

It's good to be prepared.

I need a new hiding place
for my money.
Maybe at Olivia's.

Timothy Tells Me to Forget About Mom

Says my pizza money
would better serve me
as a college fund.

But the point of money,
the only point of
anything,

is to take care of people you love.

I tell Timothy,
You'd be better off, too,
if you ditched
your dumb daughter and
stopped paying
child support.
Left her
like my dad
left me.

As It Turns Out

Olivia
doesn't like me to
buy roses
with my paycheck.

But we have fun walking
around downtown
in the cold
giving the roses away.

She tucks one
in a homeless man's
wool blanket.
Gives another to a cop.

Olivia
is not afraid
to talk to cops.

Timothy's Daughter

I finally meet
Jasmine.
Tiny.
Runny nose.
Muddy tutu.

But when Timothy sees her
it's like a light
goes on inside him.

His silver dreadlocks shine.
His silver eyes glow.
His smile
keeps turning
into laughter and
when he laughs,
his ribs dance.

The Bible

Olivia tells me I can keep my money
at her house.
She gives me
the Bible
her parents gave her
for First Communion.

Hide your money
in here,
she says.
She slips a five
between the pages.
No one will look.
Who's going to read the Bible
in this house?

Olivia's Room

is a pigpen.
Papers and dishes all
mashed in
with work shirts.
Feather boas.
Oreo boxes.

She points
to a spot
on a bookshelf
between a dead fern
and a pink sock.
Sets the Bible there.

If I'm not home
and you need
money,
just ask someone
to let you in.

Olivia's Kitchen

smells like cinnamon
and hot beans.

Dylan's at the table
drinking a root beer.
Hey, man, he says.
You here for the meeting?

I thought he hated Olivia.
He thought
$15-an-hour meetings
were fancy or stupid.

I don't know what to say.
So I kneel down
and pet the white cat
that lives here.

The White Cat

weaves away
from me.
Olivia's housemate
picks her up,
lets her tangle
her white paws
in his long black beard.

He says, *Y'all need to start
squirting fake blood
over every pizza you sell.*

Like blood diamonds,
Dylan says.
Only blood pizza.

Blood Pizza

I think of Mary's red cough
and cracked hands.
I think of
the purple
bruises Paul left
on Mom's arm.
I think of the pizza ovens.
How much it hurts
to get even the tiniest burn.
I think of those old-time factory ladies
burning to death.

I think

blood and pizza,
bread and roses.

Spring Is Colder Than Winter

because it is wetter.

Slush
goes right through my shoes.
I can't feel my feet
by the time I get to work.

Hey, Mary, I say.
I watch her ponytail whip.
Did you leave your car running
in the parking lot?

Mary turns red.
Says, *Just go clean the toilets, kid.*

We haul cardboard
out back to
the wet recycling
pile. Dylan's beard
has grown thicker and
now he wants
to major in pre-med.

When we pass
Mary's car,
he knocks
on the window.
Three little kids
pop up. They
roll down the window.

Dylan gives them
mints from the counter.

Olivia Is Crying Behind the Pizza Boxes

She wipes her tears
on rough Casa napkins.

I keep one.
I know it's creepy.

But I stuff it in my apron
pocket anyway.

Say,
Olivia, what's wrong?

It's Mary, she sniffles.

couldn't pay rent
because she
missed her
shifts. So then
she got evicted
and no
shelters have space.
And if she can't
give her kids a
home, Child Services
might take them
from her.

Oh,
Zekers.
It's
so
sad
and so
real.

Olivia sobs.

Olivia Sobs

but Mary
whirls around
Casa, yelling:
Watch your
cheese lock,
Hannah.
Wipe down
that counter,
Timothy.
Were you
raised
in a barn,
Zekers?

Her teeth
flash, her ponytail
snaps.
She hollers,

That's too much
meat
on that pie,
Dylan. You think
Casa's made of money?

Quietly and Without Anyone Noticing

Hannah turns a hunk
of dough into a perfect
pizza crust.

She drips sauce
carefully over the crust.
Works
drop by drop.

Until suddenly
in the center
of the crust
a rose—
tomato red,
bloody
red—
blooms.

When she takes it out of the oven,
Olivia starts crying again.
Says,
Hannah, you're an artist.
Says,
Look, everyone.
Bread and roses.

Overtime

CRUNCH CRUNCH CRUNCH

Scott's in his office,
making the schedule.

Mary says,
Scott, I need overtime.

Scott snorts.
Uses a high, girlish voice
to make fun of her.

He says,
I need a sick day.
I need overtime.
I need this. I need that.

His voice goes low.
He grunts.

Says,
It's not my problem.

Gives everyone a piece
on a napkin.
Gives a big piece to Mary,
saying,
You know you're hungry.

Mary's eyes are hard,
but her mouth goes soft.
She snaps up the rose pizza.
Dips it in ranch.
Eats.

I Make a Mistake

with some pepperoni.

Mary takes the mistake-pizza
to her kids
waiting in the car.

Olivia tries
to get Mary to take
a few bottles of
Coke, too.
But Mary draws the line
at Cokes. Explains:

*We get dough
and cheese and meat
at cost.
But our profit margin
on bottled beverages
is very narrow.*

Action

Olivia and Dylan
are doing an action
next month
with Burger King workers.

They'll walk off the job
during dinner rush.
Stand downtown
on strike
with signs
demanding
fair pay.

Scott found a flyer.
Says that
if we go
we won't have
jobs to come back to.

Trash Duty

I started
double-bagging
the trash at home.
A habit
from Casa.

It's a good thing, too.
The outer bag rips
on the stairs.
Only one thing
falls out.

It looks
like a thermometer.
Only it's not.

It's—

Oh God.

A pregnancy test.

Is Mom
having a baby?

Blue Way?

More like
Far Away.

I'm too mad
to go back
inside.

It's cold and raining
but I take a walk.

Stomping
through puddles.

I like babies
fine.
But a baby
will tie Mom
to Paul
for years.

I Know What to Do

When I walk past Casa,
I see Mary's car
in the parking lot.

Inside,
three little kids
crowd
around the glow
of a phone
while rain
splats.

Suddenly
I know what to do.
There's only one thing
that can make me feel better.

The Bible.

Beard guy
answers the door.
The white cat
clings to his black beard.
Beer foam
clings to his mustache.
Go on up, he says.

There's no answer
when I knock.

I twist the glass knob.
Push open
the door.
And there's Olivia
and Dylan
kissing.
His hands
in her wild red hair.

They Don't See Me

It's like
I'm invisible.
Only this time
being invisible
doesn't feel good.

I tiptoe in.
Grab the Bible.
Run.

Take the cash.
All $400.
Throw the Bible,
Olivia's present
from her rich parents,
in the gutter.

Rainwater
rolls over it,
golden
in a sudden sunbeam.

Invisible Again

At Casa
I slip in the back door.
Grab an empty
pizza box.
Stuff the cash inside it.
All $400.

Outside
rain thunks
on the box lid.

Mary's little boy
opens the car window.
Smiles,
missing two front teeth.

A delivery? he asks.

Something for your mom,
I say.

Crap

I have to work
with Olivia
today.

I could
just not
show up.

Lose my
job. Why
do I need it
if there's no way
to get back
to Blue Way?

I'm not going.

Then I hear
Mom puking
in the bathroom.

Gross.

I go to work.
Get there late.

late before.

Never seen
Scott bite his nails
before. We've never
run out of banana peppers
before. I've never
been in love
before.

Also. I wanted
to, but I never

punched Dylan
in the mouth.

Never asked him
if Olivia's
rich lips
tasted salty
from salting in.

Never wished
I'd never met her.

Olivia has a cold sore
on her lip.

*Small
miracle*, says Timothy.

(He's talking about
Jasmine's inhaler.
But I think it fits
for a cold sore, too.)

He lays mushrooms out
on a pizza
to make a dollar sign.
Then the number
15.

Wait, I say.
*I thought you didn't want
to join the fight for fifteen?*

He says,
There's a lot of things
I can't do anything about.
My ex's sleazy boyfriend.
Jasmine's asthma.
But in this case
I can be
the man I want to be.
I can stand up.
For myself.
For Mary.

CRUNCH CRUNCH CRUNCH

Scott is standing behind us
nibbling his nails.

But Timothy
doesn't shut up.

Timothy Gets Louder

So what if I get fired?
There's plenty of crap jobs
with crap pay
and crap bosses
in this town.

Scott spits
a strip
of fingernail
out of his mouth.

It lands
in the Cambro container
with the chopped
onions.
What did you say, Timothy?

You heard me,
Timothy says.

I Nearly Trip Over Hannah

She's hiding
behind the stacks
of pizza boxes.
She's drawing cartoons
on the inside lids
of each box.

The cartoon
is a sad face
vomiting
on a pepperoni pizza.

Beneath the picture
she writes,

Did You Know
We Don't Get Sick Days?
#Fightforfifteen
Or Eat Puke!

Dylan Is Whistling

His arms are
up to the elbows
in blue dish
water. I check
his lips
for signs
of a
cold sore.
But his beard
is too thick.

When he sees me,
he reaches out a wet hand
for a high-five.

But I just stand there
wishing he couldn't see me.

while cleaning a stay-over
at the motel.
Hurled pink
right into
a guest's cowboy boots.

She tells the story
while flipping pancakes.
She tells it
like it's funny.

Paul laughs.
Folds a big pancake.
into his mouth.

Says,
Huh. I'm going to be a dad.

Mary Is Living at the Elk Horn Inn

She pays $60 a night
for a peed-on
king-size bed and a dirty
microwave.

My $400.

Three weeks' wages
will last one week.

Mary's begging
for overtime.

I give her a shift.
So does Olivia.
So does Dylan.
Then Scott says,
Enough.

Dylan throws
a pepper
at Olivia.

Olivia dumps
ice
down the back of Dylan's
green
work shirt.

That's it, princess,
he says.
Picks her up.
Swings her around.
She squeals.
Her feet
knock over
the trash can.
Onion skins
fly everywhere.

Olivia! Timothy snaps.
*Aren't you the one
who wants all that
respect?
Straighten up!*

Quietly

Dylan sweeps up
the spilled
trash.

Quietly
Olivia restocks
the soda cooler.

I breathe
quietly.

Chop mushrooms
quietly.

Never heard
Timothy
speak up
before.

Quietly
Mary dries
her hands
on her apron.

She gives Timothy
a big
thumbs-up.

Scott holds up
a pizza box.
Opens the lid.
There's Hannah's
cartoon, stained
with grease.

*Customer complained
about this,*
Scott says.
Very upset.

Timothy says,
How upset?

Scott crunches twice
on a pepper.
Says,
Excuse me?

Timothy stands up.
Says,
*Get real.
They ate the pizza.
How upset
could they be?*

I Hide in the Walk-In Freezer

Shivering.

So Olivia
can't offer me
a ride home.

Walking is good exercise
anyway.

I find Hannah
in the freezer
waiting for me.

She gives me an ice cream sandwich
from 7-11.
She's been keeping it cold in there
all day.

First Day of Spring

Mary uses Olivia's phone
to find a shelter.
Finally gets a bed
at a place downtown
across from the courthouse.

Hustle, people,
Mary says,
ponytail wagging.
Once you get behind,
it's hard to catch up.

75 and Sunny

The day of the action,
Olivia rolls by
just to pick people up.
When Scott sees
her BMW,
his mouth falls open.

Olivia raises an eyebrow.
Says,
Beautiful day for a protest.

Dylan, Hannah, and Timothy
pile in.
Zekers? Olivia says.

I turn around.
Go back inside.

Slammed

Burger King.
Arby's.
McDonald's.
Subway.

All closed
due to the strike.
So everyone wants pizza.

The printer
drums out
order tickets
nonstop.
They pile up
on the floor
like snow.

Hurrying from
prep area to
oven, oven to
counter.
We cover the white tickets
with saucy red
footprints.

Get in the Zone, People

Mary says,
cheese flying
from her fingers.
She spins
pepperoni
like quarters,
each round
landing neatly
on the raw pie.

She slides it into the oven.
Then pulls out
a fresh baked Veggie Queen.
Slices and boxes it.
She moves so fast
her ponytail
stands straight up,
electric.

We Run Out of Pizza Boxes

I cut my finger
folding more.
Trying to work fast.

Then we run out of sauce.
I cut my finger
on the huge can lid
trying to
wrench it off.

We run out of peppers.
I would've cut my finger
trying to slice them.
But thankfully
the knife was too dull.

Hungry Customers

don't like waiting.
They jam up
the counter area,
pointing at us.
Saying, *Is that my pizza?*
That's a Meat King.
Is that my Meat King?
Mary stares them down.
Scolds,
You just be patient.

Scott and I
work as fast as we can.
Cheese is flying everywhere.
Hurry!
Scott yells.
Forget about cheese lock.
It's an emergency!

under the strain.
Doing toppings
with one hand.
Shoveling peppers
in his mouth
with the other.

We push pizza
after pizza
into the oven.
I stink like sweat
and spilled olive juice.

Once I slip
on pizza grease,
dropping an extra-large
in front
of the customers.

The Fog of War

I quit hearing the angry customers.
Only hear
crunching
crunching.

It sets a rhythm.
A flow.
Scott and I prep and bake.
Mary boxes and sells.

Two hours later,
face sliding with sweat,
voice rough,
Mary says,
Oh my God.
We sold four thousand dollars'
worth of pizza
in two hours.

I made $14.50.

And when he does
he inhales
a chunk
of pepper.
Starts to
choke.
His face
turns red.
He grabs on
to the prep counter.
Mary's
far away.
She's yelling
at a customer.
Ponytail bobbing.
Scott
turns purple.

I May Act Invisible

but I pay attention
in health class.
I do what I have to do.
Get behind Scott.
Wrap my arms
around his belly.
Grip.
Squeeze.

I don't see the pepper fly out, but Scott

falls
forward
suddenly
breathing
breathing
breathing.

Five Thousand

We're at five thousand!
Mary brags.

More like $21.75, I think.
We're at $21.75.

Scott wipes
his mouth.
I think of Mary's
Bloody Valentine.

But Scott isn't
coughing blood.
He just ate peppers too fast.

He says,
Mary, get me a Coke.
She runs to the cooler

and I walk off the job.

Wait!

Mary yells.
We just got an order
for a hundred pizzas
for delivery
to the courthouse.

Scott spits
his Coke.
What?
He points at me.
If you walk out that door, you're fired.

Covered in Pizza Sauce

like a soldier
covered in blood,
I walk out of Casa de Pizza.

I saved my boss's life.
Then he fired me.

I keep walking.
The sun warms me.
Red tulips
pop in the yards.
Hip-hop rolls
out of open car windows.

I'm heading downtown
covered in blood.
(well, sauce)

People stare.
Their eyes
make my body
feel light
like I'm carrying
balloons.

After an Hour

an old red Honda
waiting at the light
honks at me.

The driver
wears a Casa cap.
It's Bud,
the ancient
delivery driver
with the white and yellow beard.

He gives me a
thumbs-up.

He speeds away,
listening to Metallica.
Pizzas piled
in his back seat.

The Sun Is So Warm

I roll up my sleeves.
Catch sight of myself
in the window
of the Payday Loans.
Bare-armed and bloody,
but bouncy,
basking in the sun.

Suddenly
it's dark.
There in the shadow
of all the tall
downtown buildings,
I get goose bumps.

Then I hear
cheering.
Like our team just won.

I start running.

Pizza Court

When I get to the courthouse,
I see a huge crowd
roaring.

Bud's in the middle,
passing out pizzas
for free.

Everyone calls him
Santa
because of his white beard,
red Honda,
presents.

is across the street
from the courthouse
in an old church.
Black bricks.
Busted stained glass.
Little kids
on the broken steps.

A boy
with a headless doll
smiles
when he sees me.
No teeth.
Mary's son.
I wave.
He salutes.

I Round Up the Shelter Kids

Yell, *Everybody line up!*
Five, then ten kids
hold hands.
We march
across the street.

When they see the kid parade,
the crowd
goes wild.

I grab a box of pizza.
Pass out slices.
The kids get sauce on their faces
from eating while smiling.

Olivia Cinderella

Wearing a fancy pink ball gown
and a sparkly crown,
Olivia
jumps onto the hood
of Bud's Honda.
Yells,
Let them eat pizza!
The crowd
whoops.

But hearing Olivia's voice
feels like biting into
an olive
and breaking my tooth
on a pit.

Maybe I should go home,
I think.

Someone Taps Me
on the Shoulder

When I turn around,
it's Hannah,
hiding her eyes
with her hair.
She's made a banner.
Red paint
on a roll of brown paper towels.
I take one end.
She takes the other.
We stretch out the banner between us.
It says,
BLOOD PIZZA.

I've Seen Her on TV

but in person
the newswoman
is tiny.

*Can I ask you some questions
for the evening news?*
She points
to my apron.
Great costume, by the way.

It's not a costume,
I say.

Great answer,
she says.
Then, to the cameraman:
Did you get that?

Don't Look at the Camera

She sticks a microphone
in my face.
Says,

Don't look at the camera.
Look at me.
Can you tell us about
why you're here today?
And what is Blood Pizza?

I talk to the reporter.
Speak into the mic.

You know you're eating
blood pizza
when the people who make it
live in homeless shelters.
You know you're eating
blood pizza
when the people who make it
can't take a sick day.
Cough up blood
on the counter.

says the newswoman.
Which pizza place
do you work at?
Is there really blood
in the pizza?

I look at Hannah.
She smiles weird.
Sticks out her
front teeth
like a mouse
and squeaks.

Yes, it's true,
I say.
And there's mice, too.
I work at Casa de Pizza.

The news doesn't show
Olivia
standing on the hood
of the Honda,
saying, *Let them eat pizza.*

They show me
in my apron.
Saucy.
Saying,
Blood pizza.

The news story
isn't really about
paying better wages,
which sucks.

It's about gross stuff
that gets in food.
Like mouse poop.
Too bad.

Watching the News
with Mom and Paul

Mom screams.
Jumps
up and down
on the couch
like a little kid.
Saying,
Zekers!
Zekers,
is that really you
on the news?

Paul says,
Don't bust the couch,
britch.

But Mom is too excited
to hear him.
She jumps
and jumps
and oops,
kicks Paul in the head.

being fired.
Having so much time.

I used to lie in my bed.
Stare at the ceiling.
Practice being invisible.

Now I'm just bored.

I miss the warm
ovens.
The ringing phones.
Even Mary's ponytail.
I miss it.

Paul jumps back.
Paul is afraid of people who don't
look like him.
So afraid
he lets Timothy in to see me
without asking any questions.

Scott got fired
after that news report
went viral,
Timothy says.
I'm manager now.
And I need a real expert
in cheese lock.
Can I offer you a job?

we didn't get $15 an hour.
Yet.

Maybe
Olivia didn't love me back.
But
she got me to fight and
maybe
fighting
is winning.

Maybe
Mom will never leave Paul.
But
I can leave them both. And
maybe
Hannah and I will make mad cash
selling Blood Pizza T-shirts online.

We already have like 50 orders.

No One

gets in trouble
for calling in sick
anymore.

I make $9 an hour,
the most Timothy could get me.

But we're still having meetings
to plan actions,
battle actions
to fight for bread
and roses.

Not just us.
Other fast food people, too.
We meet at Casa
right after close.

The fight for fifteen
smells like pizza.

Mouse House

That girl. Mouse
house girl.
Hot cocoa
in the snow
girl. Freedom
fighter girl.
Quiet girl.
My
girlfriend?

Maybe.
Kind of.

At school we eat lunch
in the park.

I tell Hannah about Blue Way, about
standing on a frozen
lake.

She tells me about
Oaxaca, Mexico, and
baskets full of flowers,
wild marigolds
in November.

Lunch Dreams

Hannah and I share
a spoon to split
a pudding cup.

I tell her
about how I lied to my mom.
Said I was at
Nature Club
when really
I was working.

Nature Club
sounds like something
you'd like in real life,
Hannah says.

Like, field trips and stuff?
I say, handing her
the spoon.

Why not?
she says.
Let's make it happen.

is a real thing now.
No joke.
Hannah and I
asked Mr. Leo
the bio teacher
to be advisor.
He can use the school van
to drive us out of the city
into the woods.

Let's go, bird nerds,
he says, and drives six of us
out of the city.

Out of the city,
and into the forest.

Hannah and I
take a winding trail.

The air
smells crisp
like
where I'm from.

Bright circles
of light
shine through
the leaf canopy.
Leaves tremble
so the forest
looks like a
game
of hopscotch.

Hannah takes my hand.
My heart jumps.
There in the leaf-light,
in the pine breeze,

it's like
I'm back in Blue Way.

Only better.

WANT TO KEEP READING?

If you liked this book, check out another book

from West 44 Books:

DREAMS ON FIRE
BY ANNETTE DANIELS TAYLOR

ISBN: 9781538382479

Bidwell Academy for Girls Admission

Prompt:
What's Your Dream?

I dream
watching stars burn.
I dream blazing truth.
My dreams are
singed, charred,
scorched, and seared.
Fifty-cent plastic lighters
littering streets
fade hope's pathway.
But I
dream eyes open,
fingers on keyboards,
finding chords, dreaming melodies.
Finding words.
I dream goals,
gleaming glittering glowing.
Lighting moments.
I dream spirit building,
souls lifting,
hopes thunder.
With pens, with pencils,
I'm writing my dreams on fire.

ABOUT THE AUTHOR

Max Howard loves woods and words and finds them both in books. Max has worked lots of day jobs including pizza delivery driver, fashion show stagehand, and AP test scorer, but still finds the time to write for kids and adults. Currently, Max is writing a picture book called *The Book Formerly Known As Barf*. This is Max's first novel.

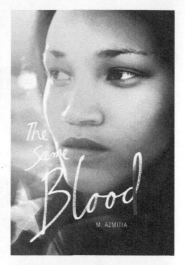

Check out more books at:
www.west44books.com

An imprint of Enslow Publishing

WEST 44 BOOKS™